William M Upcraft

Yachow and Burma

The escape, the return

William M Upcraft

Yachow and Burma
The escape, the return

ISBN/EAN: 9783337239855

Printed in Europe, USA, Canada, Australia, Japan

Cover: Foto ©Andreas Hilbeck / pixelio.de

More available books at **www.hansebooks.com**

PREFATORY NOTE

SZE-CHUEN is the westernmost province of China, bordering on Tibet. The American Baptist mission in this province was opened by Rev. Wm. M. Upcraft, who had traveled extensively through Central China distributing the word of God. He encountered in this work many dangers— once, like Paul, being stoned and left for dead outside the city walls. The mission was begun in 1889, with the station at Sui fu. Kiating and Yachow were opened later.

In 1893 Mr. Upcraft visited many churches in this country and secured reinforcements for the West China mission. Just following the Japanese-Chinese war, and possibly in some remote way connected with that war, uprisings against foreigners began in various parts of China in the early summer of 1895. At Kucheng, a number of missionaries, eight or more, were killed. The missionaries were not hated on account of their religion, but simply as foreigners. The literati and official classes stirred up the credulous mob. Our missionaries were all driven out of West China. Some came East, but Mr. Upcraft and Mr. Openshaw abode still on the eastern edge of Sze-Chuen, and after a visit to the mission, made their way through Tonkin and around by sea to Burma. They have since left Burma, and by the time this book comes into the readers' hands, they will doubtless be back again in West China and once more at work.

FRANK S. DOBBINS.

MAY, 1896.

YACHOW.

YACHOW AND BURMA

YACHOW—THE ESCAPE

IN June, 1894, a raft pushed out from the "west water gate" of Kiating, bearing as passengers Upcraft and Openshaw, forerunners of the coming workers for the King in Yachow.

The intervening year had been a time of blessing and expansion—a year indeed to be marked with capital letters in our experience, first, last, and all through. During this time also, you have learned at home to repeat the name and pray for the new station at Yachow, as month after month brought fresh leading and new development. So it continued to be with us till less than a month since—our hold upon the people and favor with them being unquestioned. A light, the light that shone where hope was born, lay along the path ahead.

And then the change came. Suddenly as the tempest sweeps over a summer sky, ill-timed as death at the festal board, it seemed to us, came the turn that drove us from our homes and made us wanderers and refugees in the land where we were wont to be styled "teachers" and "instructors." Now life is one large interrogation point : Why?

The details of all the rioting and trouble will have

been learned before this reaches you ; I shall therefore only attempt a connected story of the Sze-Chuen riots, so far as was known to us, mainly as they concern the interests of the Missionary Union.

The trouble commenced at the center of civil, military, and literary power—Chentu—the provincial capital, an enormous city lying in a vast fertile plain, at the heart of the great province. Expanding mission effort in Sze-Chuen has touched especially the work at Chentu, and the past few years have seen a remarkable increase both in agents and agencies for all phases of Christian work at that center. Medical, evangelistic, and educational enterprises, together with the special lines of women's work, have been vigorously pushed by three great societies, and all seemed to promise well for the future.

True, there had been ugly rumors afloat for some time previous to the actual outbreak—rumors of the old kind, of baby-killing and eating, of malpractices in medical work, and other slanderous reports. All this indicated a spirit of hostility, latent no doubt, but still there ; yet no alarm was felt, no danger apprehended. Whatever may be true of other fields, the missionary in China finds himself the object of constant suspicion and ill report ; thus a little more or less of that is not liable to disturb him. The gathering of the people on any public occasion is always a favorable opportunity for the display of this chronic ill-feeling ; numbers seem to lend courage in such a case, so that when, on May 29th, the feast of the fifth moon brought out all the loafers and rowdies, excited with wine and play, it was a foregone conclusion that they would attempt any mischief that might appeal to them and none more readily than trouble with the foreigners.

It was toward evening of that day that the first symptoms of coming trouble occurred. A mob attacked the front gates of the Canadian Mission and finally burst their way into the courtyard. Here they were met by two determined Anglo-Saxons, whose courage was strengthened by the knowledge that behind them were wives and children likely to become the sport of the rioters unless the latter could be frightened away. Hastily sending off messengers to the yamen asking aid from the mandarins, these two men kept the mob off for three mortal hours and then in the darkness had to take women and children and run for it. But where to run! Outside the back gate of their premises there was a near cut to the city wall, and under cover of darkness they escaped to it, while the rioters poured in at the front gate, looted the premises, and finally burned all they could not carry off. Midnight brought a respite and the mob went home to rest while the fugitives found shelter in another mission house as yet untouched.

The next morning the work was renewed. Place after place fell, the missionaries being driven from point to point till a temporary shelter was found in the magistrate's house, and even there the crowd pursued them. So the story goes, too long to be fully told here, too wide-reaching to be ever told perfectly. The genius of the rioters led them to do the most extraordinary things in order to delude and inflame the people. Fifty years ago a French Catholic priest was beheaded in Chentu, and the remains were buried beneath the Cathedral.

To-day his bones were exhumed and paraded before the populace as evidence that foreigners *kill* and *eat* people. Evidence undeniable ! Chickens were killed and their blood spattered around on the walls and tables of the dispensary as ocular demonstration of the charge that missionaries abuse their medical skill in destroying infants for evil purposes. What wonder then that the people should burn the odious houses where such evil was perpetrated ! It was thus the malign influences of the Western barbarians were banished from Chentu, and those who did it grew in both riches and reputation.

Had the fury burned itself out here, the other half of the story would not need the telling; but it is in the nature of evil to propagate itself and this instance was no exception to the law. Scattering themselves in bands, the ringleaders of the riot carried the fire into other communities, large and small, till it seemed that a reign of terror had been inaugurated throughout the entire province.

Kiating never seemed more peaceful than the day on which the news arrived there. The workers of our Western China Mission were planning for enlarged work and there were prospects of blessing. At this time the city was full of students for the triennial examination, a critical season in our work always. The effect of the reports soon made itself felt and in a few days all the mission premises were looted and the missionaries were either in the yamen or fleeing down the river. Our friends got away safely, leaving behind their home and work to the mercy of the rioters, who appeared to have made a clean sweep of things in general.

Sui fu was soon in an uproar, and though the local authorities did their best to allay the excitement, the force was too strong for them, and here again our workers were compelled to flee in order to avoid a worse fate, leaving all in care of the officials, who promised to do their utmost to preserve the premises from violence. By latest reports we learn that the houses were not destroyed, though some damage was done and some things were carried off. Just how much this means we cannot now determine and must wait till it is possible to return and make up reports later. Kiating and Sui fu, the two older stations of the mission, are thus accounted for in this narrative.

But what of Yachow, the newest and remotest of the places occupied? For several weeks prior to the occurrence at Chentu matters had been shaping themselves into permanent form. The ladies, Mrs. Hill and Miss Bliss, were on the ground and were just beginning their work for the Chinese women ; a new chapel for preaching was about completed and everything was bright and promising. The first baptism in the upper waters of the Ya had taken place, the first communion in Chinese, the first Christian marriage, and the first Christian home had been established ; indeed, the beginning of things generally had passed, and the outlook was most hopeful. Such was the aspect of things on Sunday morning, June 2nd, in Yachow. Just after breakfast that morning, a friendly official, who has been of help to us often, called in to apprise us of the news that had just arrived from Chentu, of the disorder and rioting against the missionaries, and the fear that the trouble might come to us. It was disquieting news and an ill preparation for the little morning service ; but still everything seemed so peaceful with us that we could hardly credit news so full of foreboding. In the course of the afternoon the report was confirmed and we ourselves were asked to keep quiet about it. We held a solemn yet confident prayer meeting that evening, thanking God for having brought us to Yachow and anew placing ourselves and the little work in his Almighty hands.

On Monday the Chentu affairs were the talk of the streets, the tea shops, and yamens, but every one assured us that no danger was to be expected in Yachow. Our friends came in to see us and we were reassured. News also came up from Kiating that matters were quiet there and no present need for alarm. Tuesday and Wednesday passed with varying experience. Now the reports were assuring, and again we were disturbed by threats and had to face the question of our position and responsibility. The ladies had no wish to leave, indeed were strong in their desire to stay, or at least to stay as long as any one could do so, and if we must go, that all should go together. Thus matters stood on the afternoon of June 6th, the question still undecided, when the officials called upon us again, and it was plain to be seen that they feared the worst might happen. It was after this that we decided to leave, and set about securing a few articles which, together with the silver, we felt we should need on the road. A raft was hired and preparations were completed for leaving next morning, none dreaming but we should have ample time to do this before anything would be attempted against us.

FAMILY AND OFFICERS OF CHINESE MILITARY OFFICIAL.

It was the night of the full moon, the sky being clear, and the whole blue arch unflecked by a cloud. The daylight seemed to continue later than usual, and curious, expectant groups of men hung around the door. Our every movement was watched, while in looks and manner we seemed to read the deeper intent of the heart. All acted toward us as if something unusual was expected to happen to us.

As the evening wore away, when usually no one would be about us, knots of men gathered in front of our door and time augmented rather than diminished the number. They tried to get in by the door but were foiled, and presently began yelling and hooting. The moment had come for action, and found us but partly ready. Mr. Hill took up Chester (his baby boy), Mrs. Hill and the rest of us had each a parcel of silver, and we beat a silent retreat to the farther side of the premises, where already ladders had been prepared, that we might get over the boundary wall into the next garden, and thence into the Taotai's yamen (the chief official residence), which had been decided upon as the common rendezvous in case of emergency. As we stood there listening, fearing, waiting for the entrance of the mob as the signal for our final move, a noise of a different kind attracted our ears, and presently Tzmei, our devoted young helper, came running in, with relief sounding in his very tones as he said, "The officials have come, the officials have come"; and sure enough, as some of us went out into the lane to look, there were the official lanterns, burning as fiercely as Chinese candles can burn, so placed as to form a barrier across the mouth of the lane leading to our house, and the officials themselves driving back the people, expostulating with them, shouting their orders to disperse and not break into the place.   It was a glad message to take to the waiting women in that little Chinese house —that help had come and we need not resort to extremities.   Such an experience, such a crisis, drives out all distinctions and compresses into enduring oneness the varying units of earth's scattered family.   Two American and two Chinese woman were in the little room that served as bedroom in Tzmei's house, the presence of each being a help to the others, till in sorrow the parting words were uttered that separated them, ere the work had scarce begun.

"At the fourth watch they are going to attack the house," was the challenge that met us, a challenge to faith and patience, as we sat out the slow-drawn night watches, not very confident as to the issue.   The third watch had sounded along the streets, and everything seemed quietness itself, when anticipating the rioters in any move they might be planning to make, the city officials, with soldiers, policemen, and a great retinue of coolies, came to escort us to the raft and so away from Yachow.   It was hard to leave the home just formed, the work but just begun, and that one young disciple— Tzmei—to go out, not knowing when again we might see the place ; but it was our present duty.   The soldiers with lanterns, spears, tridents, and other old world war-furnishings, fell into step behind us, as we paced the deserted streets.   Down our street we went, and were just turning off for the big north gate, Openshaw and I walking side by side, he armed with a repeating rifle and I with a hurricane lantern, when just where the shadow of house-eaves fell upon the street, staining the moonlight, we saw two clinging forms, and knew the voices that called out timidly "Good-bye, teacher." They were those of the same two Chinese women, come out to see the last of the fugitives being escorted from their chosen work and abode.

The first faint flush of coming dawn suffused the eastern sky as the raft was pushed out from the shore, leaving behind the clamorous police and coolies, who would have taken our last penny in return for alleged services and help rendered, so true is it that a man's extremity is a Chinaman's opportunity.

Escorted by a small official and some thirty soldiers we began the down-trip with mingled feelings of joy and uncertainty. The river never looked prettier, nor the rapids more exhilarating ; even our circumstances could not wholly rob us of the pleasure of such a ride. The raft with its swan-like motion, the clear sparkling stream set in the mountain freshness would have been full of delight, if only our relations with the people had corresponded with our touch and sympathy with nature. Our serenity however received a rude shock on arriving at Hung Ya, the first county seat below Yachow.   Stopping to "relieve guard" by a change of escort and report our arrival to the mandarin, we learned the disquieting news that a riot had taken place here the previous day, during which the Roman Catholic hall had been destroyed, the native Christians' houses looted, and terror spread among all those who were known to belong to the Way.   A modern version this of a New Testament incident.   It was soon noised abroad on the streets that a contingent of refugees from Ya had arrived, the effect being to draw out an ever-increasing crowd of scornful, menacing onlookers, ready for mischief at the first opening.

After waiting for some time, during which our passport was copied, we announced our intention of pulling out without an escort, deeming our alleged protectors to be our most serious danger.

"No, no, don't go yet, wait for the soldiers," was the reply we were prepared to receive, but after some persuasion our captain poled his raft out into deep water, the stream caught her, and soon we were speeding down the river.   From this point our flight was a race.   We determined to shake off our escort and avoid all stoppage at towns along the route.   Chinese soldiers and escorts generally are excellent things for show and parade, but are likely to be the first assailants in case of a row, where plunder is the probable result—hence our anxiety to be rid of them. For the next fifteen miles we had a quiet run till we reached the customs barrier at Kia-Kiang, where it is usual to leave our Chinese card with the official as an evidence of our good faith, and to enable the raftsman to pass free of duty.

All was well in this respect. We had satisfied the customs clerk and were just about to pull out, when a small boat dashed up, and a man sprang ashore, commanded us to stop, enforcing his demands by seizing our bow oar and carrying it ashore. This was a declaration of war, and needed prompt action. Openshaw jumped ashore and threw the oar back on the raft, when the man assailed him, threatening to strike. Upon seeing this I also jumped ashore and landed a convincing slap under the intruder's right ear, by which he lost his balance and fell over into the water. Bradshaw pushed the raft off and all the rest seized poles to get the old craft out into the current and away from the shore and crowd as quickly as possible. Seizing the rope by which the raft had been moored they attempted to haul us into shore again without avail, and soon we were beyond the reach of danger from stones, though not so far away but we could hear with painful distinctness the cursing and threats hurled after us by the defeated and exasperated crowd at the landing.

Failing to frighten us, our raft captain was threatened and ordered to take the raft into shore, and had there been but one foreigner instead of four of us, the attack at Kia-Kiang would have had a different ending. Cowering in sullen fright, our crew were the most abject of mortals, and not till we were so far away that recognition was impossible would they consent to work the raft. Why? Because of the tender mercies of Chinese officialdom! Had they aided us to escape, the cruelty of a Chinese yamen would have been meted out to them with an unstinted hand; but we took the responsibility along with the danger!

That night we moored in a lonely spot, just above a long, shallow rapid, the three fellows of us making a bed among the pebbles on the shore, the others occupying the raft, till a thunder shower broke over us in the middle of the night and drove us all beneath the shelter of the raft matting.

Early next morning we were under way, anxious about Kiating and possible complications there. We had sent on a man who was to travel during the night, and find out how matters stood, then meet us at the customs station above the city and report to us.

"Pull down the matting and hide all signs of our being foreigners," was the order of the day as we drew up at the well-known landing, where happily it was too early for many people to be around. With a white face and a deprecating air Lao Yie came hurrying aboard, saying in an excited whisper, "Don't stop here, they are against you now. Every foreign house is destroyed and the people are fierce"—and we pulled out again smartly. Hiding all beneath the mat cover we urged the men to row fast past the city. As we came oppo-

GROUP OF KIATING NATIVES AND MISSIONARIES.

Page 18

site the house where, less than a year before, we left
our friends in such happy circumstances, we eagerly
looked to see the home of the Vikings and their work.
A little lower down, the river sweeps in close under the
city wall, and here we saw a crowd of well-dressed men,
evidently waiting, and when the raft came opposite, we
were hailed and ordered to stop ; but, thank God, the
men proved true and stanch, pulling steadily and
strongly till the raft swung out from the mouth of the
Ya river into the larger stream of the Min, and Kiating
lay behind us.

The question of a boat in which to continue the
journey down the river was one that occupied us, the
main object being to avoid delay. Happily, in God's
good providence for us, a relative of our present raftsman came along with a small boat, nearly empty, a
bargain was struck, and in about half an hour we were
again en route. This time Sui fu was the objective
point, our ignorance of its present condition being as
profound as was previously the case in respect to Kiating.

Passing a market town—Ma-liu-tsang—in the late
afternoon, our attention was called to a crowd of men
in front of the Roman Catholic hall, which here stands
facing the river bank. A riot was in progress, and as
we passed we saw men carrying off the household
goods—a mirror especially, catching the rays of the de-
clining sun, gave back a tell-tale gleam. About eight
o'clock we pulled up at Ni Chi, in order to get pro-
visions and firewood, and sent Lao Yie ashore to recon-
noitre and report, with the result that we soon got our

men aboard and pulled out into the moonlit stream, with as little display as possible, there being "several tens" of men in the village on their way from Kiating, to arouse the citizens of Sui fu against the foreigners.

ONE OF THE FIRST CONVERTS AT SUI FU AND HIS FAMILY.

There was not much rest for us again that night. The boatman snatched a brief hour's respite and renewed the journey, so that we were within sight of Sui fu by seven o'clock on Sunday morning, June 9th. Here we had no scout ahead, but our uncertainty was soon dissipated by the kind advice volunteered by a boatman bound up river. Seeing we were foreigners, evidently bound for the north gate landing, he called out to us, "Don't go in there, they don't love you any more. Get past the city,"—advice we followed with as much celerity as possible. The boatman here proved a little refractory and demanded to stop at the east gate, saying he was engaged to go to Sui fu and would not go farther,

THE UPCRAFT BOAT ON THE YANG-TSE KIANG.

Page 21.

though we offered him extra cash to go a little way below the city where we might find another boat and get
away expeditiously. Finding he would not go, we again
assumed command for a little and so rowed past the
city without attracting attention.

Less than a mile below we tied up to look around
and determine what next could be done. This was the
home of the Hills' cook, who seemed so anxious to get
ashore we feared he meant to desert us, an injustice to
the boy, as we soon learned. After a brief survey he,
Lao Wang, came back and reported that there was a
boat moored across the river that looked as if it might
suit us. Going over we found Mr. and Mrs. Faers and
children, of the China Inland Mission, who had been
driven from Sui fu and were anxious to go down the
river, but had some trouble with their boatman. Again
provision for our need by a loving Father's hand was
apparent, and we joined forces with the Faers gladly, a
relief to both them and ourselves. There were three
small rooms on the boat. The hinder one was taken
by our ladies (Mrs. Hill and Miss Bliss) and Master
Chester Hill, the Faers family camped out in the
middle room, while the rest of us, Hill, Bradshaw,
Openshaw, and I, took the front stateroom—dining
saloon, social hall, and playground by day, its uses by
night being divided intò guard room and sleeping apart-
ment. Some objection was urged by the boatman
against an immediate start, but our company had so
much increased, we felt able to carry out our own orders
if necessary, so we insisted on prompt measures and
were soon on the way to Chungking.

How strange it all seemed, Kiating and Sui fu both threatened and deserted—all our work involved in this one fell sweep !   It was disheartening and provocative of

MR. AND MRS. MILLWOOD, OF SUI FU.

the feelings that express themselves in stinging words ; but there was little time for reflection, a constant watch being necessary, lest some careless step on the boatman's part bring us into collision with the shore people, who now seemed to be our enemies.   As the undermanned boat came slowly down the river reach above Li Chuang, one of the roughest spots on the river, the boat drew suspiciously near the lake shore, and in spite of repeated warnings not to land we steadily drew nearer till the boatman threw off disguise and said he must stop to get more men before he could possibly go on.

Meanwhile the keen vision of watchers on the shore had spotted us as we passed the town, and now seeing the boat drawing in to shore, the word was passed along and a crowd started along the bank to overtake and possess the boat in hope of plunder—a hope that came so near realization we feared at one moment that all was lost. Seizing the bamboo poles, and calling on the boatman to head her out for the center of the river, we labored at the old boat, and got her midstream and so clear of danger from the shore, when our attention was called to a boat load of men bearing down upon us. "They are only going down river and intend to cross our bows" said one ; but we were soon convinced of their real intention. As they came bow on directly for us, the foremost boatman seized a garment that hung at the side of our craft and attempted to board us, but seeing that we were too many for them at that point, the leader ordered the boat to drop astern of us, and board us there. "Take the rifle and stand them off, Openshaw ; don't let them get aboard anyhow," was shouted, and well the direction was obeyed. Bradshaw was already at the stern, and soon a cry arose, "They are destroying the rudder," thus attempting to board the boat and render her helpless at the same time. Seeing the condition of affairs, the rapidly augmenting shore crowd seized another boat and put off a second load to aid the one attacking us. It was a critical time, changed in a moment however, when the report of the rifle rang out, and the cowardly crowd rushed to the stern of their own boat, frightened by that one evidence of our ability to resist their attack.

The shot had struck the water beside the boat, the intention being only to frighten them off, not to harm in any case, and the ruse was entirely successful. The other boat stopped dead, shipped its oars, and finally drifted to shore, while the attacking force made for the shore, threatening dire vengeance upon our boatman because he had failed to aid them as they wished. Placing a guard in the stern of the boat the rest of us took a hand at the oars, suppressing the signs of incipient mutiny among the crew, and soon rounded a turn in the river and so made the best possible time from Li Chuang.

Among the truly thankful congregations of that summer Sunday, place the little crowd of fugitives on that crazy Chinese boat, when toward evening the wind dropped and we had safely passed the towns of Lanchi and Kiang-ngan, having met with no further molestation. The aids to worship were conspicuously absent, but the incentives were never stronger.

We passed Luchow next morning. It had been deserted by the mission force, the home sealed up by the magistrate, the sign and name removed from the front door, and the erstwhile "Gospel Hall" treated as the house and home of convicted criminals. To such strange ends is Chinese official power diverted. Early in the morning of the 12th we overtook the boats containing our Sui fu contingent together with Mr. Beaman, and so our forces were again united. All were well, though suffering somewhat from both heat and the continued strain, but none had suffered harm save Mr. Beaman, of whose serious adventure we now learned. It appears that he had stayed behind at Li Chuang to await our coming, hoping to be of assistance to us if, as they expected, we were on the road down the river. While escaping on his boat he was aroused at midnight by a party of armed robbers, a part evidently of the same gang that attacked us, who came bent on mischief. Taking in the situation at a glance, as the robbers were coming on the front of the boat, Beaman slipped under the mats, over the side, into the water and hid beneath the boat as long as he could hold his breath, the men meanwhile searching for him, pushing the spears down into the water to find him if possible. Coming to the surface the men quickly caught him, and some called out to beat him, but this the leader would not allow ; so contenting themselves with stealing his silver, clothes, etc., they ordered him to go across the river with his boat and wait till morning. Next day he left without delay and joined the Sui fu party farther down, thankful, as we all were too, that no further harm had been sustained, though the nervous shock in such a case is the most serious side of it.

Arriving at Chung King we found the city in a very apprehensive state, the British consul being peremptory in his orders to British subjects, and strong in his advice to American citizens, especially to women and children, not to enter the city but to continue the journey to the coast with the least possible delay. On consultation together this seemed to be the wisest as in some ways it was the only course open to the majority of our party. Such a going forth we had not expected. ''Spoiled of the Egyptians'' the little host went away, though with longings unexpressed for the work, the homes, and the few native Christians left behind. In all some forty-six adults and nineteen children went from Sze-Chuen, as the result of the disorders that originated on that May evening at Chentu.

And the future is not certain. Back of the question of indemnity for the Society and personal losses, lies the more important principle of our status in this interior country. The time has come for definition and faithful dealing with China. She must be held more rigidly to her word, and no excuses accepted for the violation of her trust. Too long other nations have been content to live on suffrance here, while granting to China many privileges she denies to them. It will remain a blot on the fame of so-called Christian nations —Russia, France, Germany—that they shackled the hands of Japan and for selfish ends bolstered up China in her attitude of sullen isolation. China should be thrown open to unrestricted foreign intercourse, instead of the grandmotherly pocket concession system now in vogue. It is a disgrace that after nearly a century of dealings with Western nations China is practically a sealed land in many important respects. Freedom of navigation and commerce with the defined right of residence to every properly identified individual would make a new order of things in China.

Missionaries are not clamoring for war or gunboats. They ask only that the rights of Americans be recognized, defined, respected ; beyond that they will occupy their own sphere for their own mission as God shall give them strength and blessing.

And does some one in the shadow of a half-defined
fear ask, "Is all lost then? The work, the prayers,
the hopes, the expressed convictions, the giving, and the
plans for coming years—are these all gone?" It needs
but a moment's consideration to find the answer in the
question itself. The work already done cannot be lost,

A CHINESE SCHOOL.

nor prayers, nor hopes, nor consecration of the means
to God. These are already garnered beyond the
danger of being lost. And the work yet undone, the
plans yet unfulfilled, the hopes of widening blessing,
these all remain, one common heritage and joy. Ask
of Bunker Hill and the four hundred slain; ask of
Bull Run and the slaughtered thousands of those fate-

ful days, Is all lost? America is the answer. Ask for
the work in Burma. But just begun, the initial dif-
ficulty scarcely conquered, the fettering language hardly
acquired, reinforcements but newly arrived, and only
scope for forward work—thus Adoniram Judson looked
upon the slow results of years in the delta of Lower
Burma and hope took a deeper hold. Yet scarce had
the larger inspiration been born, than government hostility, official interference, and the deadly breath of
cholera assailed the little band, and in the place of
numbers and song, we see one frail woman holding the
ground alone, her tenure ever being threatened. Yet
that all was not lost is attested by a far-reaching chorus
of praise to-day.

The rainbow of promise hangs above the tears of dis-
appointment and sorrow to-day and forms a call to grip
afresh the strength of God's unfailing might. Stone
Stephen, recruit Saul ; the loss is matched by the gain
in time's transforming hand.

God is waiting to win over China. We can't grow
weary till he is tired—therefore patience !

> That we may so forecast the years
>   To find in loss a gain to match
>   And stretch a hand through time to catch
> The far-off interest of tears ;

It is our attitude now in the place of servants to wait
for God.

PART II

BURMA—THE RETURN

THE land of Burma ! There is a charm in the very name, the land of pagodas and peacocks, the land of Judson, of Boardman, of Koh-tha-byu, of the deathless experiences of Ava and Oung-pen-la and two generations of richly successful Christian work.

It lay before us in the afternoon light, as the steamer "Lindula" made her way into the mouth of the river, past Elephant Point and up to her mooring beside the long wharf that forms the water front of the city of Rangoon.

There was a buzz of excited interest, pointed with many exclamations, as two Chinese missionaries made their modest way over the gang-plank toward shore. What a strange medley of faces—the brown of the Burman mingling with the darker hue of the Indian, and a dash of Chinese yellow thrown in to offset the pale faces of the Anglo-Saxons ! And stranger yet was the medley of tongues, among which our Chinese was useless!

A gharry quickly conveyed us to the Baptist Mission Press, to receive a hearty greeting from Mr. Phinney, the superintendent. An illustration it was of all the welcomes afterward given us in all the places visited in Burma.

The mission assembled in prayer meeting that evening was a rich experience for us. There was D. L. Drayton, a veteran of eighty-seven years ("eighty-seven

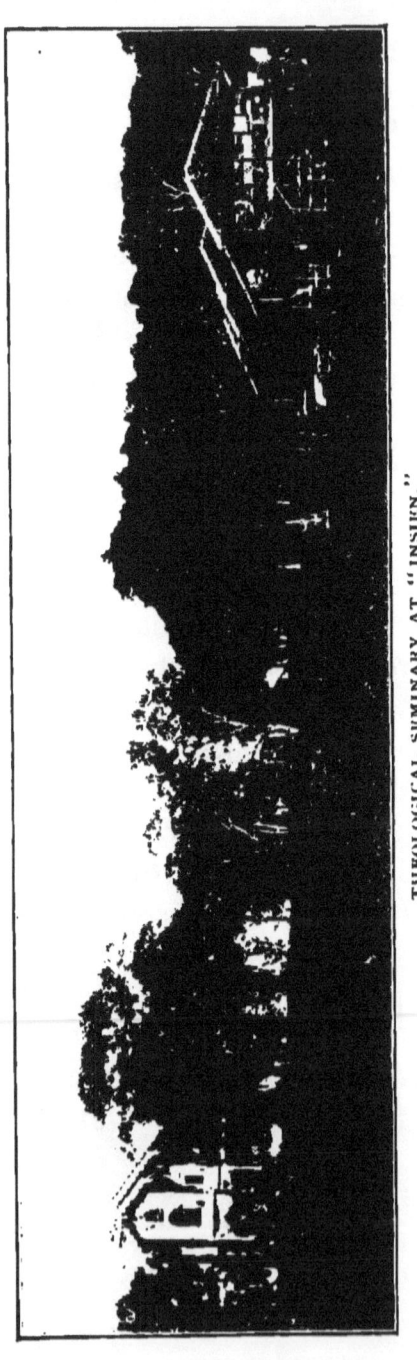

THEOLOGICAL SEMINARY AT "INSIEN."

years young'' as some one remarked), so well preserved, so sunny and hopeful, confident in faith as he still pursues the work begun nearly sixty years ago. A. T. Rose was there, whose life has been given to Burman work, and J. N. Cushing, the translator of the Shan Bible and present principal of the Rangoon College, men whose lives are history and their companionship a blessing. And others too were there, younger but honored for their work and faith, a goodly assembly of fellow-workers, larger than we had expected to see, yet needing reinforcement if the work is to be adequately carried on.

Rangoon is a composite Oriental city under the pressure of Occidental civilization, and a first-rate center

for mission work.   Missions to Burmans, Karens, Telu-
gus, Tamils, and English, are being cared for by the
Missionary Union, in addition to the institutions for
higher education, the theological seminary, and the important publishing house, a trio of far-reaching enterprises.

By the kind invitation of Dr. Cushing we met a
crowded meeting of students and other Christians at the
college a few nights after our arrival, who assembled to
hear something of China and the recent doings there.
A more enthusiastic and responsive audience no speaker
ever had, and when later Mr. Gilmore brought report
of the subsequent action of the College Church in
donating its funds to the Lord's work in Western China,
our hearts were full.   " How much can we give ? " was
asked, and thus the answer came, " Give all we have in
the treasury,'' and we were richer by so much plus the
stimulus to faith and humble joy imparted by the terms
of the gift.   No offering ever made a deeper impression
upon us than that spontaneous, unlooked-for donation
of our Burman brothers in church meeting assembled—
a model offering indeed.

Many doors were opened to us in Rangoon and many
sweet tokens afforded us of the divine blessing.   The
Lanmador Burman Church had just dismissed its morning service the first Sunday in December, and was pre-
paring for the session of the Sunday-school, when a
welcome cry announced the coming of the Chinese
teachers.   Good souls, how glad and eager they were !
And they imparted much of their own spirit to us as we
looked into their faces and briefly saluted them in the

c

name of their Lord and ours, and then grasped hands—
eye speaking to eye when no common tongue speech
was known to us.   And that night their offering was
brought to us, to be supplemented later on by a sum
almost as large again—an "abounding in liberality"
that caused us much joy and encouragement.

From this gathering in the upper room we hurried to
the Baptist church, where was a gathering of warm-
hearted Christians from the districts around Madras,
under the care of Mr. Armstrong.   There had been a
reconciliation between some dissentient members of the
church and this was "making-up" day, the feud being
healed.   Auspicious day for such a message as we were
there to bring !

"Speak slow, sir," said the aged pastor as we stood
side by side; "speak slow, because I don't understand
English much."   So we began our mental service to
the appreciative, patient gathering before us ; but only
for a little while, when some unusually long, hard sentence in the strange, difficult English tongue brought
the pastor to a full stop and we sought the service of a
younger man from the audience to take his place.

Then the handshaking, the indispensable accessory to
every meeting, and then the—no, not the collection,
but a committee to obtain free-will offerings for the
Chinese work—a committee on soul expansion in its
most tangible form.   A new meaning was being acted
into the word and thought of "fellowship," and to us
"brotherhood" was being amplified and emphasized.
This singularly blessed day closed with a couple of meetings in English, which gave us the freedom of our

mother tongue and contact with the sons of mothers far across the sea.

It was Christmas morning and Christmas wishes were being passed. With them came a tiny square envelope, prettily ornamented by a love-guided pen, addressed "To the mission-aries from West China," and with it a roll of rupees and some much wished for por-traits. But why rupees? Inside that envelope, within a carefully designed border of daisies, you may read, "Please accept 'in His name,' the free-will offerings of your brethren in Christ." "In Christ," and therefore the "feeling togeth-

PAGODA.

er" that so truly expresses itself as coming from brethren.

The pride of Rangoon, from a Burman's view point, is in the delicate and much-worshiped Shweydagon pagoda, whose gilded spire is everywhere visible in a

Rangoon landscape. But beneath the slowly changing form of external Buddhism a new force is being introduced and beginning to work, that shall finally supplant this idle, helpless system with the realities of faith and love made common to men in Christ.

From the Irawadi to the Salwen, a day's ride on the steamer, is a transition in a large sense.

Moulmein is the antithesis of Rangoon. Quiet in habit, classic in setting, the difference is one of disposition and circumstance. A noisy, jubilant, bustling youth is Rangoon—a sedate, complacent, attractive spinster is Moulmein. The environment of mission work here is of the most desirable order, and the corps of workers is in happy congruity with the work and setting.

To meet and know the parents of Ah Sow and Ah Syoo was a privilege highly prized, and we look upon that large, active Christian home as a new annex to our heritage of friendships. Chinese in origin, Burmese in development, these have grown into a sphere of faith and work beside which a crown or a mitre is but a bauble.

Hanna, Sara, and Tien Sie, children of Ah Syoo, the head master of the Moulmein Boys' School, came to greet us the evening of our arrival, and quickly broke through the barrier of strangeness and made themselves at home with us. "Sing to us, Hanna," was a request quickly obeyed, as the three little ones ranged themselves in line, their black eyes sparkling with delight, to sing in Burmese, Karen, and English, "Jesus loves me, this I know," to be followed by the same strain in Chinese, in our rough men's voices, less suited to the simple harmony and words perhaps, though no less ap-

preciative of the confident, comforting truth of Jesus'
personal, protecting love.

Boys and girls, men and women, Burmese, Karen,
and Anglo-Saxon, vied with each other in showing kindness to the "China missionaries" for his sake whose
Spirit makes our unity more than an empty name.
Money they gave who could ; some whose ability in this
direction was too limited to satisfy their desire brought
handkerchiefs and picture cards for work in China.

A feeling of gladness for their love, of honest pride
in their work, of sadness at the parting—a feeling com-
pounded of many emotions, and one to be often repeated in the succeeding days, had entire possession of
us, as the faces on the wharf faded into indistinctness,
with the growing speed of the steamer down the Salwen.

Away off there on the left, as we reached the point
where the river mingles with the sea, lay Amherst, the
resting-place of Ann H. Judson, the heroine of our
earlier years, the sainted mother and tireless worker,
now better appreciated as growing years reveal the
fuller meaning of the missionary's toil.   Peace seemed
to rest upon that charming spot, peace and hope
wrapped around by the morning sun.

"Can you go at night, captain?" was asked, when
one evening we found ourselves on the steamer headed
for Bassein, in narrow and sinuous creeks, bordered by
dense jungle, with here and there an opening to the
paddy fields beyond.   Night navigation to our lands-
men eyes seemed a certain way to disaster ; but later

when the electric search light was turned on, waking
the slumbering birds and starting them upon a reckless,
unheeding flight, or attracting armies of winged insects
which fell upon the iron awning with a rattle like hail,
we found ourselves in a dual world, the old world of
Burma streaked across with lines of a new world's light.

Our happy experiences at Bassein need a book to
state them in detail.   Renewed contact with men whom
we had known in America, the touch with the Karen
work in its most complete development, the eager interest of the Christian assemblies, the promise in the
schools, in the saw-mill, in the growing confidence of
the churches, all this and much more can only be indicated in the roughest outline.

The day after our arrival (Saturday) we spent in the
jungle.   A Karen home received us.   The venerable
owner gave us a large welcome, and as recent experiences were related, and features of the "wild
tribes" on the Chinese hills delineated, the old man
drew closer yet to the interpreter, his eyes aglow and
lips held in suspense apart, as he recognized point after
point in the family likeness, and affirmed with emphatic
nods, "Yes, they are our people"; and then like old
Simeon he wanted to see with his "own eyes" the
members of his ancient family.   Strangers in Burma,
their native hearth is in another realm, even as the
origin of Americans must be sought across the sea, and
it was impossible not to sympathize with the Karen in
his eager recognition of the old home, and his desire to
reconquer it in the force of divine love and bind it
with faith's golden chains about the throne of God.

And it may be that such a consummation is soon to be achieved. The Sunday in Bassein was a full day in every sense, from our hearts outward. Burman service at 7 A. M. with Mr. and Mrs. Tribolet (he interpreting), then meeting with Pwo-Karens, our dear friend Cronkhite as interpreter, and later the Sgau-Karen gathering with Mr. Nichols as mouthpiece to a splendid assembly of Christian culture and intelligence. One side gallery was occupied by the local Chinese, attracted by our blue gown and pigtails—"allee samee Chinaman." But alas! their knowledge of English did not serve to convey religious intelligence and they left early; but the Karens untiringly listened, till across the bridge of speech we found the common ground of brotherhood and hope. It was a good day, such a day as a sower seeks in spring.

"You will find missionaries here and money for their support when you need them for work on those Chinese hills," Nichols said, when together we had talked with a group of the elders on the veranda of the mission house the following day, a prediction easy of belief as he handed in a little roll of coin from "two Karen women," an offering augmented later on by a handsome donation, the fruit of Karen love and solicitude for the welfare of the hill tribes across the frontier of Upper Burma.

The stars were out in marshaled order in the sky as we left Bassein and its beloved circle for Henzada, getting just a peep at Maubin by the way. Two days' jungle trip revealed to us some of the special features of Karen work. In company with Mr. Price we went from vil-

lage to village and met with the Christians at three sep-
arate points, morning, afternoon, and evening. The
Karens have reared for themselves convenient, econom-
ical chapels, resembling nothing so much as overgrown
thatched dovecotes set up on posts, which serve as
tabernacles of assembly for the church and school
buildings for the village children, and become the most
potent force in these little communities.

The day following was Sunday ; its gathering began
at the riverside, where a strong athletic fellow from the
school was baptized in the presence of a crowd of
students and townspeople, a scene in striking contrast
to the performance at the adjacent Buddhist shrine,
where offerings of flowers, lights, and prayers are made
before the image that never nods or goes astray, waking
never from the slumber that holds the earthy form in
helpless bondage.

In the afternoon a Burman gentleman translated our
English words into his vigorous vernacular to an appreciative audience at the chapel where Mrs. Crawley
and her associates carry on a work for the conservative,
picturesque Burmese. The tints of the shapely turbans
lay in careless contrast to the deep brown faces of the
wearers, who so far forgot the supposed sacredness of
the place as to encourage the speaker with a kindly
smile and whispered comment—a style one has leisure
to enjoy when speaking through an interpreter.

Early the following morning there was another gathering by the riverside, when the Karen schools, sweet
girl voices in happy concert with the stronger tones of
the bigger lads, joined to sing us away, earning for

themselves the approval of the steamer folks in the remark, "By Jove, they can sing well, can't they?" A little packet lay on the cabin table containing pictures and "other financial accessories" from "the girls' school," a field in which an earnest, consecrated woman serves her Master among Karen girls, who in later years will be colleagues to workers yet to come.

BURMESE FAMILY—FOUR GENERATIONS.

It was hard to say good-bye to Rangoon when finally the time came to leave for the journey north, toward the home in China. So kindly had been our welcome, so ideal our relations with all our fellow-workers there, it was in a marked manner good to be there, and correspondingly difficult to get away. Mr. Phinney, our host and tireless helper, came to see us

off and give his final fatherly counsel to the two he had
sheltered for upward of a month in his home. A little
gathering at "The Press" that morning cannot be
passed in silence. A row of six foremen of differing
nationalities stood before us to receive our word of
thanks and farewell. And why? Well, there is, in the
account furnished us by the Mission Treasurer, an item
that reads "From Baptist Mission Press Employees. . .
forty-four rupees, four annas"; the meaning thereof is,
that these men, be they Christians or Mohammedans
or Buddhists or whatever else, had put this sum to the
account of "the Chinese missionaries" for their use
and work, hence the thanks—thanks not only to these,
but over and beyond them, to him, the Lord of us all.

The first stopping place on the way north was Pegu,
where we were to stay one night only, but speedily
changed the plan as we drove home with Miss Payne,
the efficient administrator of the mission work at this
point. A passing glance at the Pegu Reading Room,
revealed one of the links by which the missionary has
attached the community to herself. A bright cheery
room, "free to all," well stocked with current literature
and standard works of interest and profit, no irritating
rules, and a convenient situation—this is the reading
room, a common focus for all English-speaking res-
idents in the town, and evidence of the happy relations
existing between the missionary and the Europeans
under circumstances that sometimes provoke mutual
criticism and hostility rather than the helpfulness exerted
in the present case.

The glimpse of the work afforded to us on Sunday

showed the school gathering before the service in the forenoon, and later the church, to which we spoke, "rehearsing what God had done for us." Moung Thra din, a capable official under the English government, was interpreter, and showed his interest in old China, as did the rest of the Christians, in the help they contributed for the work of the gospel out there. Nothing has more vividly and permanently impressed us than the spontaneity and genuineness of the sympathy with the work of Christian missions to be found among the churches in Burma, and Pegu was in line with the rest.

At sunset, "in the gloaming," we had a service with the English-speaking community, one of many held since we came to the country, in which the freer utterance in our mother tongue, coupled with the larger common ground between speakers and hearers, has given us a joy and opportunity unknown to workers in Sze-Chuen.

The work at Pegu is in a promising condition, and we take it that the life of one capable, earnest woman, such as we found there, is more than an answer to the bandying criticism of the outsider, to whom missionary work and all that it represents is a matter for no more serious consideration than is afforded in a poor pun, an after-dinner joke, or a sarcastic allusion in alleged accounts of personal travels.

To get to Shwegyin involved a run by rail to a wayside station at which we found an escort and bullock cart awaiting us for the continuance of the journey. The road was dusty, the sun was hot, the bullocks inclined to self-assertion, and the cart a construction

without springs, and there were four and a half miles
of first experience of this kind of conveyance for us.
Whatever energy may have been wanting on the part
of the animals beneath the yoke, was more than com-
pensated for in the vigor and versatility of the driver,
who now scolded, now wheedled, and anon tickled the
flanks of the "mild-eyed oxen" with a rattan, or re-
minded them of their duty by a prod with the spike at
the end of his goad.

Having finished the cart ride we took a dose of
native boat, crowded in with a regiment of native passengers beneath a mat, where the smaller the man the
more comfortable the position was the rule, and so we
reached the steam launch which lay with its saucy nose
rubbing against the sandy bank awaiting her freight
for Shwegyin.   The lights of the town were twinkling
along the streets as we made our way to the mission
compound, to be warmly welcomed by our friend Mrs.
Harris, last seen in far-away Omaha.

After serious interruption, the work is now flourishing
under the care of Mr. Harris, who follows here the work
of his father begun in years long past.   The morning
after our arrival we were introduced to the preacher's
wife in words which brought back the faces of the Rangoon College students.   "This is Homer's mother,"
was the form of introduction, and right well did we come
to know her in the succeeding days.   "Homer said I
was to give it to you for the Lord's work," was her
apology for an offering she brought, to which Homer's
younger brother had added a share, and other shares
were taken, some by the school teachers, some especially

for *Chinese women*, all given spontaneously and love-prompted, and much of it having been made up before-hand.   Thus did they enhance the value of their gifts.

And Homer? He is a student under Dr. Cush-ing at Rangoon, the best all-round athlete in the col-lege, a solid Chris-tian fellow, to be a worker on the Karen hills by-and-by, we hope —such is the Ka-ren Homer.

At Shwegyin are three Chinese Christians.   What interest sparkled in their eyes as they came to speak to the teach-ers who "lookee just same belong us," and were no less glad than

A CHRISTIAN STUDENT.

themselves to speak again with Chinese where both were on stranger soil.   Not of us, but Catholics, yet glad to hear and eager to get Gospels to read in their own tongue.   "May the Heavenly Lord protect you, teachers,'' was their expressed wish for us and ours for them as they went away.

There is a large field in Burma for Chinese work, which should be promptly undertaken if we are in future years to have a hold upon the formative forces in the coming Burman ; and no others are so well able to handle this work as we in our widely spread, efficient organization at so many important points throughout the land. Natives of India and China are a growing force in Burma and must increase largely in the near future, to add a new problem to the questions of this field unless now solved by adequate measures for their evangelization.

Toungoo welcomed us with a large force of Baptist missionaries. In some respects our experience here was unique. In company with Dr. Bunker, Miss Anderson, and others, we visited a Karen Association out upon the mountains. A long but enjoyable ride by narrow paths gave us a taste of jungle travel and a sight of jungle villages in a district relatively new to mission work. Delighting in solitude, the Karens have placed their villages in least accessible spots, while their habit of removing their dwellings from place to place to suit the exigencies of their method of cultivation is a factor in obstructing the easy communication essential to rapid social development. The second day out from Toungoo we noticed boards bearing a sentence in the attractive letters adopted by the Karens, and soon came upon one bearing in large English lettering—WELCOME —our whole experience tending to prove that for us indeed we had well come. A modern " feast of Tabernacles '' was that Association, with some added features, noticeably the brass band of Karen schoolboys. The weather is a "certain quantity" here during the dry season, hence protection was only needed against the sun by day and dew by night ; no apprehension needed to be felt as to rain.

A spacious, low, grass-covered booth was erected for the meetings, fenced about with plaited bamboo, and around it were little shelters, also of bamboo and grass, for the accommodation of guests, the largest being reserved for the foreign teachers, of whom there was quite a contingent : Messrs. Bunker, Cochrane, Seagraves, Heptonstall, and "the Chinamen," with the Misses Anderson, Thompson, and Pettey, and the faithful helpers and teachers among the Karens themselves, a capable body of men reared and trained upon the field. A father among his children, an elder among his people, is the missionary in such a gathering, a position that brings responsibility and care, with much of joy and patient habit.

The consciousness of latent power, the first stirrings of approaching manhood, are now swaying the Karens here, for which much wisdom and patience will be needed in order to give right direction to the awakening power. In the process of development men generally have strength first and wisdom after, the one the dower of youth, the other the product of the years; but the latter comes at length.

The diversity of type among these mountain peoples is very marked, very marked also their uniformity in some phases, notably in the lack of soap. Various methods of personal adornment are resorted to, with an approximation to success on the part of the women, who seem to uphold the claim made for the sex in matters of this kind, and certainly evince more appreciation of the fitness of things than do the men, who, after foolishly piercing their ears, are content to insert into the expanded hole a little roll of cloth, sometimes more than an inch in diameter; but the women wear an ornament of silver that has worth at least and some charm.

A group of young men was pointed out as teachers from the Brec country. Worthy of notice are these sturdy fellows, who leave the comparative ease of the Christian villages and live away among the wilder tribes to the east, enduring hardness and doing the work of evangelists and teachers, a splendid tribute to the impelling power the gospel has brought into their lives. The position they occupy brought us into near sympathy with them, so in the missionary meeting we were able to greet them in gladness on three grounds: "First, because you are Christians; second, because you are Baptists; third, because you are missionary," their response finding outlet in the giving of what they could to the mission work in China. There is a great field upon these hills to be worked yet, a field that expands with closer knowledge; and among the Karens throughout Burma a *race* of missionaries is being developed for these outlying fields, where the few white teachers cannot go. On all the different Karen fields, Bassein, Henzada, and elsewhere, our growing acquaintance with the people and observation of their life and

habits and devotion only served to emphasize this con-
viction. The political future of the Karens may be
doubtful, their ultimate absorption into surrounding
peoples a possibility ; so much may be granted and yet
leave the real worth of the Karen as a Christian unim-
paired—his capacity for aggressive mission work and
devotion to such a life. Here we think is the true
standard of value for the Karens.

A happy morning was spent on Dr. Cross' compound,
where, in his eighty-first year, he still retains oversight
of the work. After a service in the chapel, the older
Christians gathered in a kind of informal reception at
the doctor's house, where we sat around together on
the matting. Every Karen was a living interrogation
point, and the "poor missionaries" the gladdest men
in the crowd. All were eager to know of those "wild
men" in Western China, so they dressed themselves in
their national garb and sang sweet little bits of their
home songs, always inquiring with zest, "Is that like
the Karens in China?" And a Christian woman,
thinking of her kin beyond the frontier, was moved
to make a really handsome donation, and the spirit
spread and the sum grew to large proportions. When
Miss Simons told us of it in the evening prayer meeting, our surprise and rejoicing were about equal at this
new proof of love's sisterhood to action.

On the Sunday morning, under Mr. Cochrane's leader-
ship in the Burman chapel, a united service was held of
a character somewhat unique, uniting in one rather
noisy service the Burmans, Indians, and Chinese. The
last attracted by the novelty in the speakers were

D

especially demonstrative.   Men from different places
along the Chinese coast, where dialects differ, helped
one another to understanding, as here and there the
meaning of the speaker dawned upon a mind more
acute than the rest.   "Yes, that's doctrine," they
murmured in chorus, as something struck them pecu-
liarly after their own ideas.   We shall long remember
that united service and the sweet singing of a Burmese
Christian woman.   God's blessing be on them all.   A
farewell gathering is a correct designation of the scene
on the station platform when the train drew away.

There is ample cause to be proud of the Baptist force
in Toungoo, of the capable work that is being done by
them, with a common good feeling and whole-hearted
interest in the work of God in every place.   In the
community here, as at some other points, much interest
was awakened and kindness shown, revealing the true
attitude of those outside missionary circles yet in constant touch with missionary life, to the movements in
progress around the homes where they live.   There is
a "lay missionary" family in Toungoo, whose culture
of coffee and conduct of life are of great value in the
display of Christian principles, whose hospitality to the
Lord's workers is as abounding as their sympathy is
deep.   Such have peculiar honor and reward from the
Divine hand.

"Something like a city" is the verdict on Mandalay.
By this is meant that it is more like a Chinese city than
any other yet seen.   There is a wall and moat around
the inner city, now known as "the Fort," and a gen-

ON THE IRAWADI ABOVE MANDALAY.

Page 50.

eral likeness to the style of place known to us in the
Flowery Kingdom.

The spire of the Judson Memorial Church is visible
among the trees as one approaches the mission compound, the entrance to which is by a gate at the rear of
the premises. The brick-built house and school are a
trifle heavy in appearance from the outside, an impres-

THE LYON MEMORIAL CHAPEL, BHAMO.

sion apt to be deepened by an interior view. Mr. Mc-
Guire is doing work that ought to be divided between
two men. The development of the actual work and
redemption of pressing opportunity in this great center
need better equipment.

Sagaing and the site of the Ava death prison occupied us on Saturday. This latter took us back to the
earlier steps in Burman work, with which all readers of

missionary records are familiar.   The shackles and the
lash, the fear and uncertainty, the triumph of Christian
faith and fortitude, on this jungle-overgrown spot on
which Judson and others suffered and endured—Ava,
now a name with us—these are all factors in the coming
of the kingdom of God among the Burmans.   To-day
we suffer and wait in the darkness; to-morrow we sit
in the sunlight with hope radiant.

At Sagaing is the answer of the Christian church to
Ava and its prison, where she is working through the
hands of her missionàries for the children of those who
riveted the shackles of the earlier day.

At Oung-pen-la the aged Burman preacher gave us
his blessing on the spot where the captive missionary
lay during those long uncertain months before the final
release.   See the contrast.   At Ava the oppressor lay
in ruins; at Oung-pen-la the new faith is rearing a tem-
ple in Burmese hearts for the indwelling of the Christ
whom their fathers rejected.   The process is slow at
present; a season of stone-quarrying before the build-
ing goes up.

On the journey north, where the route crosses the
Irawadi, we saw and bade farewell to Mrs. Sutherland
and her children, whose kind thought provided us with
necessaries for the journey.   These are the little
touches that give color to life.

From Sagaing a traveler occupied the same compart-
ment in the train as ourselves and asked many inter-
ested questions of us ; became, in fact, an organization
for that purpose, e. g.: "Is your father a Christian?"
"Yes."   "Where does he live?"   "America."

"How long has he lived there?" "Was he always a Christian?" and so under the impression that we were of a different descent to himself. Asking where he was bound for, imagine our surprise to find that he was only traveling a little way up the line with us in order to satisfy his curiosity about us. Finding that he was a Christian, we parted with the sympathy of kinship.

The last stage is partly by rail and partly by steamer,

KACHIN SCHOLARS.

and as during the dry season the river is very low, one is never sure of reaching Bhamo till actual arrival has taken place. As it was we stuck on a couple of sand bars and were delayed thirty-six hours, a detention that earned for us the title of "Jonahs," with the additional comment that "parsons *always* bring bad luck."

Mr. Roberts, of the Kachin mission, was on hand to

welcome and help us, and as we drove home together pointed out the mountains that lay between Burma and China, the home of the Kachins and field of the missionary's work. A feeling of home stole over us that evening as we gazed upon familiar outlines bathed in the intense blue common to mountain scenery in West China.

"Home mail," the first we had seen since last September—it is now the end of January—and then oblivion to "things present" for a little space.

The Kachin mission, with Messrs. Roberts and Hanson and Miss Stark as workers, has entered upon a career of peace and development after the stress of trial and vicissitude of former years.

The school work, together with the many phases of station and country work that is really the care of a people evolving from the jungle state, in which plunder is their profit and the traders' caravan their harvest, into Christian units with the difficulties incident to childhood, and later into communities fitting themselves to the restraints of home and trade,—all this keeps the missionary's heart and hands full of thought and labor. He is the standard of their living. "He gave some to be teachers," not *all*, but *some*, and to them is the need and promise of divine grace.

"We thank Thee for one of thy servants whom thou hast taken to thyself in the night while we slept, and pray that the son she has left may be strengthened to follow and serve thee," were the missionary's words in the morning prayer. "Who is it?" was our question when the prayer had ended. "An old woman at

Cha-yeng,'' and arrangements were already made for
the funeral to take place that day, so we went to see
and learn.

A Kachin house is a bamboo cage on posts, divided
into little apart-
ments in keeping
with the s m a l l
forms of the own-
e r s. A Kachin
village is a collec-
tion of such cages
placed with a due
regard to disorder
and distance.   A
n o t c h e d t r e e
slanted in posi-
t i o n before the
door s e r v e s as
stairs for entrance
and ''w e l c o m e
e v e r s m i l e s''
upon the visiting
missionary.

The people had
already gathered
for the funeral

KACHIN GIRLS.

when we arrived and made our way to the house with
the new presence there we call death.   The coffin, a
rough box as roughly covered with red muslin, stood
just inside the door ; a group of elderly women was
formed around a fire in one corner of the room (just

why these bamboo houses don't all burn down is a constant wonder); while behind a bamboo partition the
younger women were collected in a similar way; we can
just see them through the hole left to act as doorway.

A couple of mats were laid on the ground outside, the
coffin was carried and placed in the center, the neigh-
bors gather around in the position known as squatting,
and the missionary gives out the hymn, "There's a land
that is fairer than day," and commences the service
of comfort and hope.   A fair land is the land lying
before us, the brown of the stubble fields in the fore-
ground shading off in the nearer distance into the long
grass and waving bamboo, while beyond all are the
mountains, with the blue spread across them with opal
clouds lying on the sky's open face.

They take the loose lid from the coffin and the poor
withered face is shown on which the storm of years has
left its scars; the feet too are seen, begrimed with the
dust of many roads, but all stilled and quiet now—and
so the preacher tells a sweet story of a land fairer far
than any known to us now, and of the welcome for tired
ones who in faith may reach its rest.

She was a Christian and didn't want to be buried
among the heathen, so a place in the wild jungle was
chosen, and there they laid her in a chamber that might
well be called Peace; the missionary bent his head in
prayer while some hearts were wondering on the mys-
tery of death and what the hope of resurrection from the
dead really means to the Christian.   So helping them
in life, comforting them in death, the teacher's work
touches both sides of his people's life.

The village of Mankang lies upon the bank of a pretty winding river about twelve miles from Bhamo. Here is a chapel and orderly community of Christian people under the care of a Karen from the Bassein district, who is doing missionary work and is sent by his own people. Sunday, February 2nd, was communion day, with the monthly covenant meeting and reception of candidates. Four persons were presented for baptism, and examination was conducted early on the Lord's Day morning by the missionary and elders of the church. The first man was quite ready at reply and passed satisfactorily, being received by a unanimous vote. The second applicants were a man and his wife, seeing they both came together and wished to be so received. The man had wanted to come some time ago but the wife threatened to leave him if he did so, but to-day they came together. He apologized for slowness in answering questions, "It was not in his line," but the little woman had just that look that one sees in devotees and was much readier than he. The elders deliberated long and carefully, examining the man's recent history, asking with whom he had been "planting paddy," or farming it we should say, that being considered a true test of the man's character—how does he act in business transactions?—so step by step they unraveled the past, considered him all right and both were received, as was the remaining candidate, a widow supporting herself by farming.

The afternoon was set for administration of the ordinance. Accordingly all the village was gathered at the riverside, where with singing and prayer and orderly

decency they were buried with Christ in baptism, and
emerged from the symbolic grave to live, we trust, in
humble, loving service of their Lord.

Shiveringly they stood to receive the hand of welcome and fellowship by the water before returning
to their homes and the subsequent gathering around
the table of the Lord to "set forth his death till he
come," and then we left the little band, joined as they
are with us all who, in every place through all the
earth, meet in the unity of the faith and obedience in
like manner and testimony.

The sun was setting behind the mountains and gloom
was deepening in the forest as the missionary "allowed"
to his companions that "we are on the wrong road,"
and we began to discuss the possibilities of one horse
blanket as a covering for the three of us, when a friendly
Shan put us on the right track and helped us back to
Bhamo.   As we reached the compound the lights in the
chapel showed the work here going on as usual ; so all the
forces possible are being employed for the reclamation
of the Kachins from their present condition and salva-
tion through the gospel of the grace of God.

From Bhamo to Myitkyina (pronounced Mitcheena),
the outpost of mission work in Upper Burma, is a de-
lightful ride on the steamers of the Irawadi Flotilla
Company.   Here are stationed Mr. and Mrs. Geis,
earnest and consecrated, their home the center from
which the light is to radiate in widening circles into the
little communities of Kachins situated among the beau-
tiful hills that surround Myitkyina, and make it one of
the prettiest and most healthful stations in the country.

Everything is new, the place itself being the creation
of the English officials, from which they control a large
district contiguous on its eastern face with the Chinese
province of Yunnan. Here, as everywhere, Chinamen
are a potent factor in the life of the new community,
and numbers of them are passing continually on their

SHANS.

way to and from the jade mines, which are situated at
some distance to the west.

The Kachins are yet somewhat shy and less free with
the missionary than at Bhamo, where the work is of
longer standing and better known. Indeed, it is only
of recent date that all the ·mountaineers have been
subdued to English rule. One cannot fail to be struck
with the genius and energy of the British in their work

of colonization.   Firmly, yet considerately, they bring
their force to bear upon the chaos of native rule, and
speedily create an orderly, well-governed province, in
which the law is administered without favor and the
rights of all are secured.   So are they casting up a
highway for the Lord, and are instruments—even
though unwittingly—in bringing about his kingdom.
Order, justice, liberty, are the characteristics of British
rule in the East.

Of work among the Shans we could see but little.
Bhamo does not offer a very large field for work among
these people, though Dr. Griggs is using medicine and
education as means for reaching as many as may be.
At Namkam, an outpost on the Chinese frontier, four
days to the southeast of Bhamo, are Mr. and Mrs.
W. W. Cochrane, in the same work.   The position is a
most advantageous one for contact with the Shan people, though the station is somewhat isolated for the
missionaries.   From Namkam the natural step is into
China, and we are glad again to have our faces set toward the field in which, *while we can*, we *must* work.
There does not seem to be a choice of location in our
case, but just as long as there is opportunity and we
are free, just so long will China be our field, our home.

Looking back now upon the two months spent in
Burma, there is one dominant feeling, one outstanding
feature, and one transcendent wish for this great field.
We feel deeply and increasingly thankful for the work
and its attendant blessing.   The little one has indeed
become a thousand, and there is promise of greater increase in the days now coming.

The one feature of the field that is likely to most
impress a soul sympathetic in the work, is in the wisdom and sagacity shown in the planting and development of the different missions of the Missionary Union
in Burma.   True, there are other places, and important
ones, yet to be occupied ; but with the men and money
at their disposal, there has been a vast territory covered,

BUDDHIST SCHOOL.

an immense work undertaken, and many initial difficulties overcome.   The era of development has been
well entered upon in many places, the training of the
Christians carried out, a system of education introduced,
and most gratifying results are apparent.   Our wish for
Burma as we stand related to it is, that in the years now
before us, the wisdom, consecration, and devotedness
of the fathers may all descend upon the newer workers
and a great season of conquest be upon all the field.

To the many of our dear colleagues in the ranks of
the American Baptist Missionary Union whose fellowship we have enjoyed, whose hospitality we have shared,
whose work has been an inspiration to us, and to those
whom we have not seen, but who are more real and
near because we have been in Burma, to them all is our
love and esteem ; to each of them we say, ''For the
sake of the house of the Lord our God I will seek thy
good.''

To the supporters of the Missionary Union are our
greetings and congratulations.   You are partners in a
noble and enduring work ; the years will increase the
fruitage of your fellowship and ripen the result of your
labor.   '' Enlarge the place of your tent,'' and make
a more ample field wherein to reap.   As the sowing so
the reaping.

As we remember the Christians, Burmese, Karen,
Indian, Kachin, all of them in the brotherhood of faith
and work, whose hands we have shaken and whose
offerings have so enlarged us, we '' thank God and take
courage.''   There are a thousand rupees, the gift of
love from Burma to China—the fruit of your fellowship.
In joy and hope we thank all who have so strengthened
our hands and hearts.

The years will bring us all closer and truer in our
work and experience.   While we have grace to remain
faithful and zealous, time is our friend and the revealer
of the full import of the work of the church in her
missionary sphere.

Glad for the past, confident for the future, we cross
the frontier into old China, rejoicing that we have been

given the privilege of a little missionary journey in the footsteps of the fathers.

> Watchman, tell us of the night,
>   For the morning seems to dawn.
> Traveler ! darkness takes its flight ;
>   Doubt and terror are withdrawn.

THE END

www.ingramcontent.com/pod-product-compliance
Lightning Source LLC
Chambersburg PA
CBHW030022030726
47499CB00008B/3082